Louis

Maddie Tries to be Good

Illustrations by Marie-Louise Gay

Translated by Sarah Cummins

First Novels

Formac Publishing Company Limited
Haifax, Nova Scotia

Formac Publishing Company Limited acknowledges the support of the Nova Scotia Department of Tourism and Culture. We acknowledge the financial support of the Government of Canada through the Book Publishing Industry Development Program (BPIDP) Canadä for our publishing activities. We acknowledge the support of the Canada Council for the Arts for our publishing program.

Canadian Cataloguing in Publication Data

   Leblanc, Louise, 1942-

   Sophie devient sage. English]

   Maddie tries to be good

   First novel series)

   Translation of: Sophie devient sage.

ISBN 0-88780-482-9 (pbk.)
ISBN 0-88780-483-7 (bound)

I. Cummins, Sarah. II Gay, Mary-Louise. III. Title. IV. Series.

PS8573.E25S627513   1999   jC843'.54   C99-9850192-5
PZ7.L4693Ma 1999

Formac Publishing
Company Limited
5502 Atlantic Street
Halifax, NS B3H 1G4

Distributed in the U.S. by
Orca Book Publishers
P.O. Box 468 Custer, WA
U.S.A 98240-0468

Printed and bound in Canada.

Table of Contents

1
Battles at home

"There is a risk of severe storms today," they said on the radio. I forecast the same thing at home.

First my parents had a fight. Then my mother cut her hand when she was slicing bread. That was the last straw.

"I've had it! I'm at the end of my rope," she cried as she ran out of the room, dripping blood.

My dad decided to lie low. He put the slices of bread that mom had left in the toaster. "It seems to me that you could give your mother a hand," he grumbled and he slipped away.

I couldn't believe it! My parents have a fight and I get the blame! It's like there's no more love in this family.

My brother Julian was completely unaware. He was flipping out about something else. The little genius was going over his reading lesson, and stumbling over every word. He said it was an idiotic lesson, especially for a boy.

"D-d-daddy d-d-dressed my d-d-dolly in a d-d-diaper."

Angelbaby stopped eating, a terrified look on her face. I'd better do something quick, before she starts to scream. That would finish off my mother.

The radio was playing a catchy tune. I turned up the

volume and began to dance and clown around for Angelbaby.

"Dooby-dooby-doo. Babada-boom, Baby!"

Angelbaby was laughing and banging her spoon—PLOP! right into her bowl of cereal.

The bowl flew off the tray. I watched it sail across the room.

"D-d-daddy d-d-dressed my d—"

It landed smack on Julian's head. But that was the least of my worries. All of a sudden, the kitchen seemed to disappear in a smokey haze. I rushed to the toaster and pushed up the lever. There was nothing there. The toast was completely incinerated.

That's when my parents decided to come back, with Alexander, my other brother, trailing behind them. He was carrying his school bag, which looked like it was ready to burst open.

He refused to say what was inside. Ridiculous! My father

made him open it up. Although maybe this wasn't such a great time to make a scene ... over my jacket.

"You're taking my beaver jacket without asking?"

"You would have said no! I have to have it so I can be in the musical group at school, The Buckteeth."

As usual, Julian came up with a brilliant suggestion.

"You can borrow my jacket. It has a horse on it. Horses have buck teeth too, just like beavers. I don't need it for the play."

Great! Now he was going to be in the the drama class? He'd be bugging me all year!

"You're too little, Julian. You would just get in everyone's way."

"You just don't want me around. You're mean! Besides, if I'm so little, how can I get in the way?"

"If only I could FLY-Y-Y-Y away!" a singer on the radio was shrieking.

"My sentiments exactly," my mother said in a tearful voice. She picked up Angelbaby and walked out.

"FLY-Y-Y-Y away!"

My dad turned the radio off. Silence fell over the kitchen. It was awful.

Dad seemed to be in a daze.

"It's time for you kids to leave, too," he muttered.

Outside things weren't any better. It was pouring rain, and we could see the back of the school bus bouncing away in the distance. My dad hastily piled us into the car and drove us to the next stop.

As we got out of the car, he started to sing the same old refrain.

"You're the oldest, Maddie. You should try to be reasonable. Julian can be in the play if he wants to. Try to get along better with your brothers!"

I was incensed! Inside me a voice was crying, "What about Alexander? He steals my jacket and you don't say a thing! Everybody can do what they like, except for me!"

"MADDIE! Do you understand?"

"Yes, Dad."

But inside I was still protesting. "No, I don't understand! No one is getting along, not even you and Mom! This family has become impossible!"

Fortunately, I knew my friends would understand me.

2
Battles at school

Things were just as bad at school. Every single one of my friends was in a foul mood.

Patrick, the tough guy in our gang, practically smashed my face in after the ball game. For nothing!

He dropped the ball and our team lost the game. I told him he was a butterfingers and he got mad. He threw the ball right in my face.

"Oh sorry, I'm such a butter-fingers," he said, which made Nicholas laugh. I told him he was a monkeyface.

"Better a monkeyface than a sourpuss," he replied.

"And a heart of stone," added Alexander.

I didn't ask what they meant, but they told me anyway. Nicholas said I was being a pain in the neck.

"And she's selfish," said Alexander. "Because of her, I can't be in the musical group."

And then he told everyone about the beaver jacket incident. To hear him tell it, the group couldn't get along without him. The Buckteeth would fall apart, and it would all be my fault.

Everyone went on and on about my selfishness. Even Clementine, the leader of the gang, who is supposed to be my best friend.

"Try to be nicer to your brother. He's not going to wreck your jacket."

I'd like to wreck her! She should butt out! She doesn't

have a brother. She has no idea of the problems having a brother creates. Anyway, our private family affairs are none of her business.

I felt that I was ready to take on a starring role. I was mad at Alexander and all my friends. They didn't understand.

RRRRRING!

Finally, recess was over. Thank goodness! Next was drama class. Maybe I would be able to let out all my emotions. That's what the best actors do.

I felt that I was ready to take on a starring role.

* * *

"This is the story of Masto, an elephant with a heart of gold," explained Mrs. Pinsent, the drama teacher.

An elephant! That wasn't the kind of part I had in mind, but it was the starring role.

"Masto is an old elephant who has lived a life fraught with hardship," she went on.

Well, I could relate to that. After all I'd been through so far that day!

"Masto is a wise elephant. The younger animals in the jungle all come to Masto for sage advice."

Just like me, since I'm the oldest child!

"Each one of you will play the part of an animal who comes to ask Masto for help. Each of you must make up a story."

"Like a fable?"

"That's right, Julian."

Oh, Julian. I had forgotten he was coming to this class. He was sitting in the back.

As the others went off in groups, he approached me. Grrr ... I thought he would ask to work with me. I would say no. Then he would say I was mean. But no, he walked right past me.

He went to talk to Mrs. Pinsent and she gave him a book, *Aesop's Fables*. I figured out that Julian was going to use it for inspiration. He really is a little genius.

Still, he could have asked me for advice! He sure holds a grudge. Just like the others. Well, I didn't need anyone else, if I was going to be the elephant.

At the end of the class everyone presented their animal. Patrick, of course, wanted to be the lion, and Clementine chose to be the mouse. He'd eat her right up.

But no one picked the lead role, until ...

"I'd like to be the elephant," someone piped up.

Who was it? NICHOLAS! That guy couldn't string two words together. His mouth was always full of candy, which he gets from his dad's corner store. The only animal he could ever play is a squirrel. I had nothing to fear from him.

"I would like to be the star ... I mean, play the part of the elephant, too," I said.

"We'll decide at the next class," said Mrs. Pinsent. "Perhaps the part will go to the most deserving one."

The most deserving one? What did that mean? It wasn't at all clear to me.

3
Alone in the jungle

In the school bus everyone was talking about what Mrs. Pinsent had said.

"It's obvious!" declared Clementine. "The most deserving one is the one with the best behaviour." She is such a goody-goody.

"The class is not about good behaviour," I pointed out. "It's about drama. The important thing is to be a good actress."

"Or a good actor," Nicholas shot back. "Masto is a male elephant."

"Says who? There's no reason it has to be male. You're just sexiss."

"SexIST," Clementine corrected me.

"Oh, go back to your mousehole, little mouse!"

"QUIET!" roared Patrick, the lion. "I am king of the jungle. I will settle the question."

Nicholas and I couldn't care less and we started to argue again. I tried to make him see reason.

"I am a lot more like Masto than you are!"

"You've got to be kidding! Masto has a heart of gold. I'm a generous person because I give candy to everyone."

"You do not! You take candy from your father's store and try to sell it to everyone!"

"But I sell it cheap. And if I had a beaver jacket, I would lend it to Alexander."

Soon the argument turned into a fight. In the end, the bus driver was roaring like a lion.

"Get back in your seats! Or I'll show you who's the QUEEN of the jungle!"

There was quiet for a few seconds. Then Alexander spoke.

"I think Maddie would be perfect in the role of the elephant."

I couldn't believe it.

"For one thing, she's fat."

I really couldn't believe it!

"She's not really fat," objected Julian. "She's just plump."

23

Sniff! I couldn't ... sniff! My brothers are monsters. Sniff!

Through my tears I saw that the bus had arrived at our stop. In a heavy silence we made our way off. As soon as we stepped off, the laughter burst out. It washed over me, crushing me flat.

My heart felt as heavy as an old, tired elephant. The world is a jungle, I thought. Or a boxing ring.

I asked myself a horrible question: Is there anyone on this earth who loves me?

GRANNY! Granny loves me. I'll go live with her. I'd be much happier, that's for sure.

Inside the house, we were greeted by laughter from Angel-baby. She wasn't screaming, and that was a good sign! Maybe my mom would be in a better mood too.

Granny was there! She came! She must have guessed that I needed her. I rushed towards her.

"I have to talk to you, Gran. It's extremely important."

She didn't answer "Yes, darling," as she usually does. She looked strange. She put Angel-baby down in the middle of her toys.

"Later, Maddie. First I have something to say to you all. It's about your mother. She needs time to ... think, and to rest."

As usual, Julian just didn't get it.

"I'll go tell her she can sleep as long as she likes. We won't wake her up."

"If you go upstairs to tell her that, you'll wake her up," Alexander pointed out.

He didn't get it either. If Mom needed calm, then she must have left the house. Anybody would!

"She's gone to stay with an old friend," Gran told us.

My mother had an old friend? This was news to me!

"For a few days," Gran added.

So she'd abandoned us for a few days! That was shocking. Now I wouldn't be able to move in with Gran! I still wanted to tell her that—

"So please be good and go do your homework while I feed Angelbaby."

Grrr! I had no chance to talk to Gran all evening long. After she put Angelbaby to bed she

had to take care of Alexander and Julian. By the time my dad got home, it was time for me to go to bed.

I couldn't sleep. I tossed and turned in my bed like a fish out of water. And I felt like one too. I felt like it was the end, but I didn't know what it was the end of. I was afraid.

I couldn't stand it. GRANNY!

I got out of bed and went into the hall. YIKES! My dad was coming up the stairs, and he was crying! I didn't think such a thing could ever happen.

There must be a serious reason, that's for sure.

It must be my mom! She wasn't coming back! She told us, but no one listened to her. I could hear her tearful voice: "I've had it. I'm leaving."

I collapsed onto my bed. Now I was a fish who knew that this was the end of our family.

My head buzzed with reproaches. "You might help your

mother out. You're a pain in the neck. You're mean. Selfish."

It was all my fault. Even Granny thought so. That's why she wouldn't talk to me.

I was a poor solitary child lost in the jungle. It was awful. Way too awful.

My mother had to come back.

4
Maddie the model child

The only way to get my mother back home was to bring harmony back into our household. As soon as I got up I began to put my plan into action.

"Here, Alexander!"

"You're lending me your beaver jacket?"

"I'm giving it to you!"

"What? I don't believe you."

"Honest, it's yours."

"Something's fishy. Oh, I know! You want something for it."

"No, no, I don't want anything."

Alexander was dumbfounded. His eyebrows looked like question marks.

I didn't tell him that mom had left us forever. He was too young to bear the shock.

If I told him that I'd decided to be kind and patient, he wouldn't understand. He would laugh in my face.

Instead, I just said, "The jacket is getting a little small for me."

Suddenly Alexander blushed. "You know, I didn't mean what I said. You're not really ... fat."

I was so pleased! But I wondered whether he really meant it. Still, being generous sure pays off. People like you more.

I thought of testing this theory out on Julian. He was deeply engrossed in *Aesop's Fables*.

"Do you need any help, Julian?"

"NO!"

"Are you sure? I would love to help you!"

"I said no, billions of blistering blue barnacles!"

Julian can really stay mad a long time. I would have to be more patient with him.

"I'm your big sister. I could help you pick out your animal."

"No thanks. Granny already helped me, and she's bigger than you."

I felt like screaming, "You tried to turn Granny against me!" But then I thought about my mother and bringing harmony to our family. Plus I wanted to find out more.

"Really? What animal did you decide on?"

"Top secret, sis. I'll only tell the elephant. And you haven't shown yet that you deserve that part!"

Grrr ... sometimes a little genius is not the easiest creature to live with. Still, Julian gave me an idea. To show I deserve the part of the elephant, I would put my plan into practice at school. I would become a model pupil.

* * *

POP! Scritch, scritch.

Nicholas was so annoying with his chewing gum! Before the 'scritch scritch' there was the 'froosh froosh' of his candy wrappers. It was very hard to hear what Mrs. Spiegel was saying!

Nicholas was wasting his time and he was wasting my time too. Didn't he understand how important it is to pay attention in class, if you want to do well?

For the last two days I had been paying attention to my teacher. It made an amazing difference.

I realized that Mrs. Spiegel is an excellent teacher. Also, you can learn a lot of things at school. It was unbelievable!

During class I forgot about how sad I was. I forgot about my mother being gone, although it haunted me the rest of the time.

Grrr ... now Patrick was bugging me. He rummaged around in his desk, took out a peashooter and aimed it at Mrs. Spiegel. Surely he wasn't going to—

FWIIIT!!!

Too late. The pea shot out.

It missed Mrs. Spiegel but it hit the vase of flowers on her desk.

BIIING! went the vase.

"OH!" went Mrs. Spiegel.

The class cracked up. Even Clementine. Really, it was disgraceful.

At recess I told them all what I thought of them, how they were behaving like a bunch of juvenile delinquents.

"It was just a little pea," laughed Patrick.

"You could have injured Mrs. Spiegel."

"Her back was turned. A tiny little pea was not going to injure her. Not with a bum like hers."

Clementine laughed so hard she doubled over. Really, I was very disappointed in her! And I told her so.

"So now we have to ask your permission before we can laugh," she retorted. "What's the matter with you?"

"Yeah!" POP! "Before, you would have passed Patrick the ammunition. You couldn't stand Spiegel the Eagle."

"And now I can't stand you, Nicholas! Couldn't you stop stuffing your face at least during class? It's very distracting!"

"You're just jealous, fatty!"

"My sister is not fat!" thundered Alexander, running up.

He was wearing my beaver jacket and carrying a pair of drumsticks.

Nicholas was aghast. "You said yourself that she was—"

"If you say that word, I'll beat my drumsticks on your teeth, and you'll never eat candy again. Beaver's honour!"

"She's FAT!" roared Patrick.

Alexander turned on him, waving his drumsticks.

"Whoa there, little drummer boy, or I'll turn you into beaver stew" Patrick said. "Lion's honour."

"Let them be, Alexander," I said in a scornful tone. "Their insults won't make me change. Some day they'll understand."

"Oh, I understand already," Clementine cut me off.

I didn't like her tone of voice.

5
Maddie's lumps

Some people really have a twisted mind. Do you know what Clementine said? She said that I was acting like a lamb so that I would get the part of the elephant.

Well, okay, the thought might have crossed my mind. But now, I was behaving like a model child because I wanted to. It was just natural.

"And," Clementine added in her little squeaky voice, "she gave her jacket to Alexander to show how generous she is."

Never would I have expected such viciousness from that little mouse! And the worst thing was that I couldn't defend myself.

I couldn't tell the others what was going on at home. They all thought we were one big happy family. They envied us. Wouldn't they be pleased!

Plus I didn't want to mention it in front of Alexander. That might cause a scene.

Well, my plan failed. Like a mouse leaving droppings everywhere, Clementine sowed little seeds of discord in my brother's mind. What fertile ground!

By the time the school bus got to our house, the little droppings had turned into enormous lumps.

As he walked into the house, Alexander warned me, "Don't expect to get your jacket back if you get the part of the elephant."

"I have no intention—"

"Or if you don't get the part! NEVER! Over my dead body!"

Now there was a tempting thought! Alexander was such a pain. It wasn't easy trying to create harmony with him. Or anybody else, for that matter.

Still, I did believe that I had achieved a degree of self-control. The important thing was to keep talking.

"Could I say something, PLEASE?"

"All right," Alexander muttered suspiciously.

"You would believe Clementine, a stranger, rather than your own sister?"

"Exactly. Because I know what you're like."

That was so depressing. How could I prove to him that I was sincere? Then I had an idea. "Well, you can keep my beaver jacket and I'll give you the matching T-shirt too!"

"Will you give me your beaver cap too?"

Alexander drives such a hard bargain! Fortunately, there weren't any other matching items, or he'd clean me out completely. Just to get it over with, I agreed to the cap.

"You're right," Alexander conceded, as he carried off his

loot. "I should trust my sister more than some stranger."

I was beginning to realize that when you're too generous, people exploit you. Achieving harmony in the family was proving to be very costly. Now there was only Julian left to buy out.

He was still with Gran. I could hear the two of them laughing. I didn't like it. I was jealous. I knew I shouldn't have been, but I was.

I felt very unhappy.

Who was I kidding? My plan wasn't working at all. Despite my superhuman efforts in the last two days, I had not brought peace and understanding to our home.

I felt like a puzzle box. Inside everything was in pieces. My feelings, my ideas were all mixed up. I just didn't know ...

"Hi, sweetie!"

It was Gran! I fell into her arms and turned into a fountain. Tears flooded down my face, and I cried out my despair.

"What more can I do? Why doesn't Mom come home?"

Well, imagine my surprise when she told me that Mom hadn't left for good. I had just jumped to the worst conclusion.

"Your mother is only human, Maddie. She has weaknesses like anyone else. And a life beyond the family. Just like your dad!"

"But they never talk about their other life. How are we

supposed to know what they're going through?"

"You're so right. Sometimes people wait until a crisis breaks out before they do anything."

I recognized myself a bit in what she was saying. It was only when I was afraid of losing my mother that I decided to be good.

"That's depressing, Gran. That means that harmony is impossible."

"Not impossible, just difficult! You have to work hard at it every day."

Then she told me one of her magic tricks.

"When you're dealing with other people, try to think of them as another Maddie. You'll understand them better."

"But then, everyone else has to follow the same rule, if you want it to work."

Granny found that very funny.

"It's easy to get along with you," I told her. "You always understand me."

"Well, this time it was Julian who understood. He knew you were going through a rough patch."

"Julian?!"

"He told me: 'Maddie's got problems. She thinks she's an elephant. You should talk to her, Gran. I'm too little. She would only step on me.'"

Whew!

6
Saved by a bee

The next morning I had no problem in thinking of Alexander as another Maddie. After all, he was wearing my jacket, my T-shirt, and my cap. We got along very well!

It was a little more complicated with Clementine. She attacked me head-on.

"I hope you'll change the way you've been acting."

"What's wrong with how I've been acting?"

"It's really hard to take. Come down off your high horse and I'll explain."

"You come down off yours first."

Little Miss Perfect needed to be taught a lesson.

"If you want to talk about it, you should think of me as another Clementine," I told her.

She looked at me like a terrified mouse. I explained Gran's system to her, and she said she was willing to give it a try.

Two minutes later I was calling her Maddie and she was calling me Clementine. We laughed so much we split our sides. Then we talked about our problems.

"Just an argument! It takes more than an argument for a couple to break up. And believe me, I know what I'm talking about," Clementine confided.

"Hey there, fathead!"

Grrr ... sometimes Patrick really gets on my nerves. It would be a while before I could call him Maddie!

BANG!

Grrr ... then Nicholas popped a chip bag right in my ear.

But I could see through their little game. They were trying to make me lose my cool. Really, they were pitiful. Just poor pathetic human beings.

Very annoying human beings!

In class Nicholas chomped down twice as much candy as usual. It was an orgy, an avalanche of rustling candy wrappers.

Patrick bombarded me with peas from his peashooter. In no time I was riddled with tiny

black-and-blue marks. But I re-
acted like a marble statue.

Want to know how I was able
to resist? By reminding myself
that it wouldn't last forever.

Because drama class was coming up.

* * *

The hour of the elephant was near. Everyone had presented their little fable. Everyone but Julian.

"I will be a bee," he said. "And I will save the elephant. Just when a hunter is about to shoot the elephant, I will sting the hunter on the hand and make him miss his shot. I want to show that you sometimes need someone smaller than you to help you out."

Mrs. Pinsent almost swooned, she thought Julian was so clever.

"But the elephant needs to be really big," added Julian. "Two

people are needed to play this part."

Would he just mind his own business?!

Mrs. Pinsent went wild over this idea. And I was wild with anger at my little brother. After class, I muttered in his ear.

"Would you just mind your own business?"

"But Maddie, I saved your skin!"

"Stop pretending you're a bee! You're not living in a fable anymore."

"No, I saw Nicholas practising to be the elephant. He was fabulous. You would never have gotten the part over him," declared Julian.

I couldn't believe it. Nicholas was fabulous? Then he came up to us.

"Would you like some chocolate?" he asked sweetly.

I could see right through his generosity. After all he'd eaten, he wasn't hungry anymore. I wasn't about to let my guard down.

"Since we have to be on the same team, I suppose we should

get one thing straight," said Nicholas.

"What's that?"

"How the part is divided. I'll be the head of the elephant, and you can be the behind."

The behind! I was supposed to play the part of an elephant's behind? I had to hold my breath just so I wouldn't blow up.

I would have to talk to him, persuade him to change his mind. I tried to think of him as another Maddie. But all I could picture was another elephant. I couldn't accept it!

I was tired of fighting. In any case, I wasn't sure I could win. I needed some time to think it over.

"We'll talk about it tomorrow," I told Nicholas. "The jungle's not on fire."

I'd have to read *Aesop's Fables*. Maybe there's a story about an elephant ... with two heads!

And I'd see what Julian thinks. Because sometimes you need someone smaller than you to help you out.

Three more new novels in the First Novels Series!

Marilou on Stage
by Raymond Plante/ Illustrated by Marie-Claude Favreau

Marilou's class is putting on a play, based on an old fable. Everyone has a role, and Marilou is the star. But no one likes the way the story turns out, until the class decides they can give the fable whatever ending they want. In their new version, everyone gets treated fairly.

Leo and Julio
by Louise Leblanc/ Illustrated by Philippe Brochard

Leo's parents have left him on his own for the evening, and that means his best friend Julio can come over to visit. But there's something special about Julio, a secret which Leo is afraid to share with his parents. In the end he can't avoid telling them the truth, and to his relief his parents believe him. At least they pretend to until they give Julio a ride back to his place — in the cemetery!

Missing Mooch
by Gilles Gauthier/ Illustrated by Pierre-Andre Derome

Carl is on his way to his summer holidays on the Magdalen Islands. He remembers the islands as the place where he and his old dog Mooch had so much fun. This time Carl is going with his friend Gary and Gary's dog Dumpling. Terrified of everything, Dumpling clings tightly to Gary. Carl can't help remembering his noble and magnificent Mooch, and how she protected the beach from seagulls and swam out fearlessly to fetch sticks. The more ridiculous Dumpling becomes, the more Carl is convinced that he has to do something to honour Mooch's life.

Meet all the great kids in the First Novels Series!

Meet Arthur
Arthur Throws a Tantrum
Arthur's Dad
Arthur's Problem Puppy

Meet Fred
Fred and the Food
Fred and the Stinky Cheese
Fred's Dream Cat

Meet Leo
Leo and Julio

Meet the Loonies
Loonie Summer
The Loonies Arrive

Meet Maddie
Maddie in Trouble
Maddie Goes to Paris
Maddie in Danger
Maddie in Goal
Maddie wants Music
That's Enough Maddie!

Meet all the great kids in the First Novels Series!

Meet Mikey
Mikey Mite's Best Present
Good For You, Mikey Mite!
Mikey Mite Goes to School
Mikey Mite's Big Problem

Meet Mooch
Missing Mooch
Mooch Forever
Hang On, Mooch!
Mooch Gets Jealous
Mooch and Me

Meet the Swank Twins
The Swank Prank
Swank Talk

Meet Max
Max the Superhero

Meet Will
Will and His World